CAVE
DADA

BRANDON REESE

chronicle books·san francisco

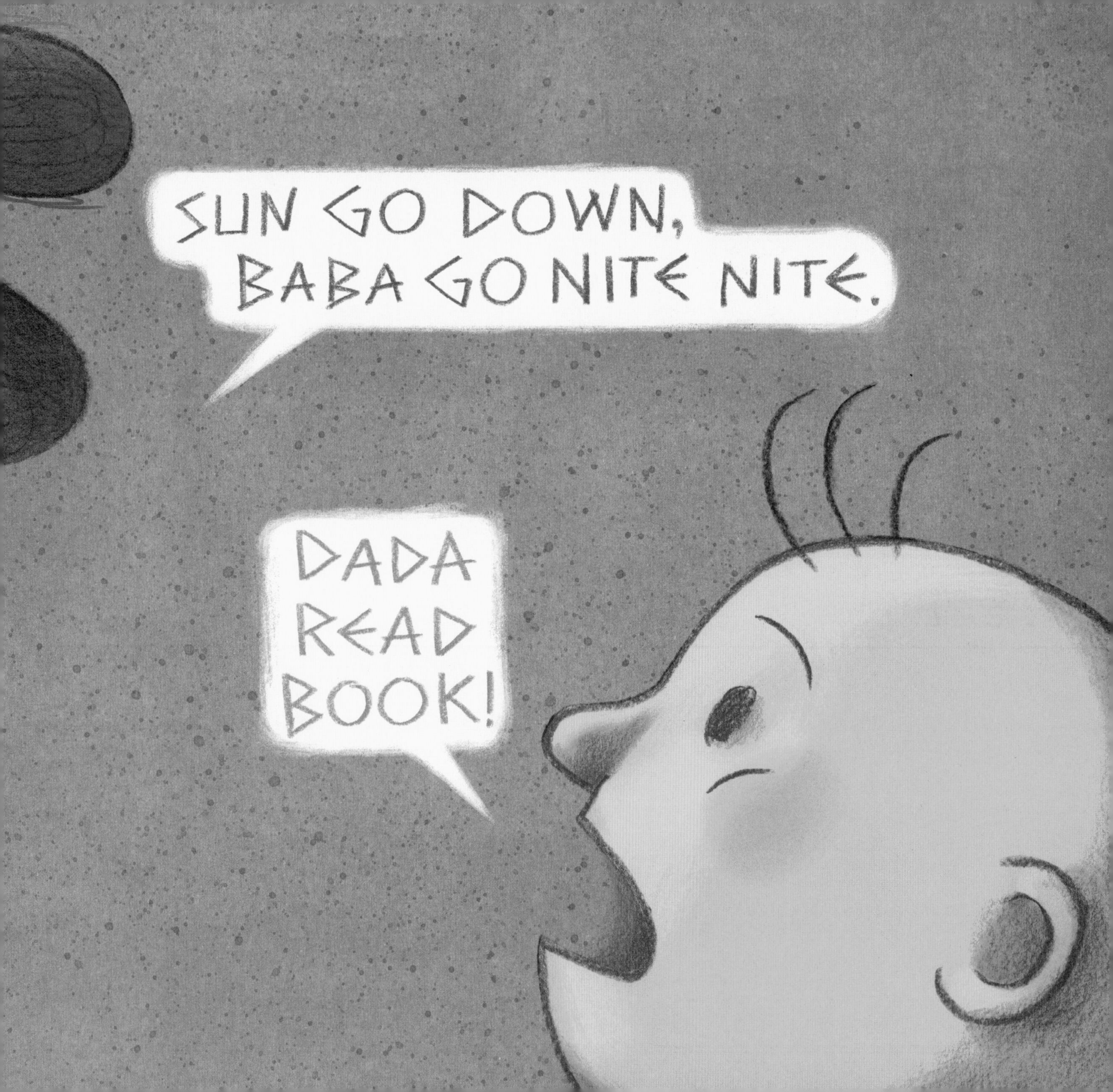
SUN GO DOWN, BABA GO NITE NITE.
DADA READ BOOK!

DADA TIRED. HUNT GATHER ALL DAY.
DADA NO READ BOOK.
UG. BABA FEEL CRY.

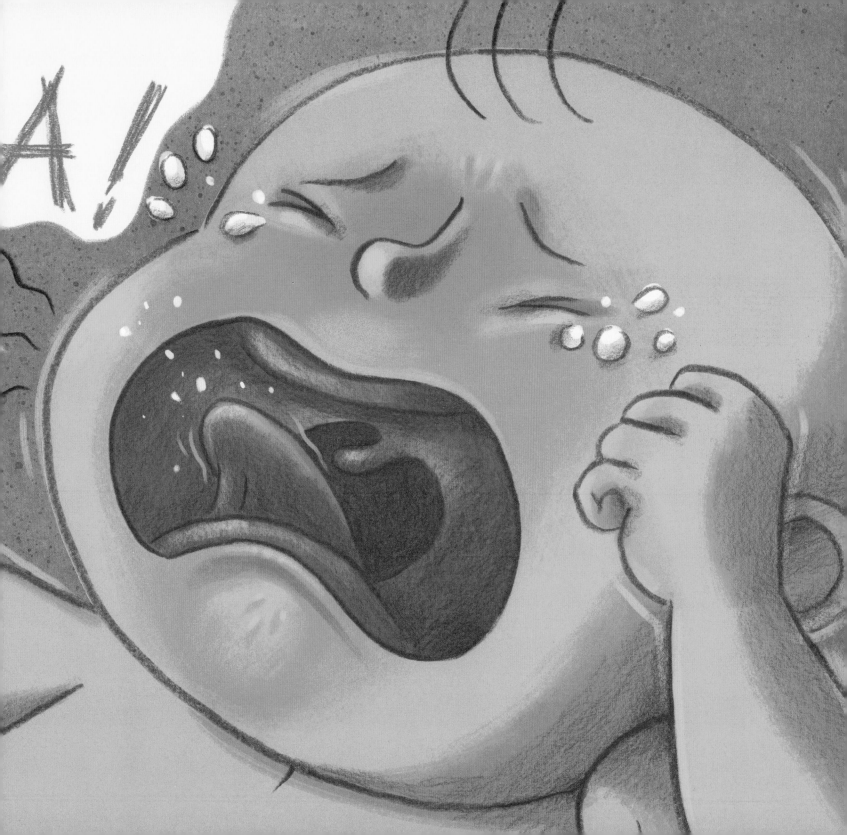

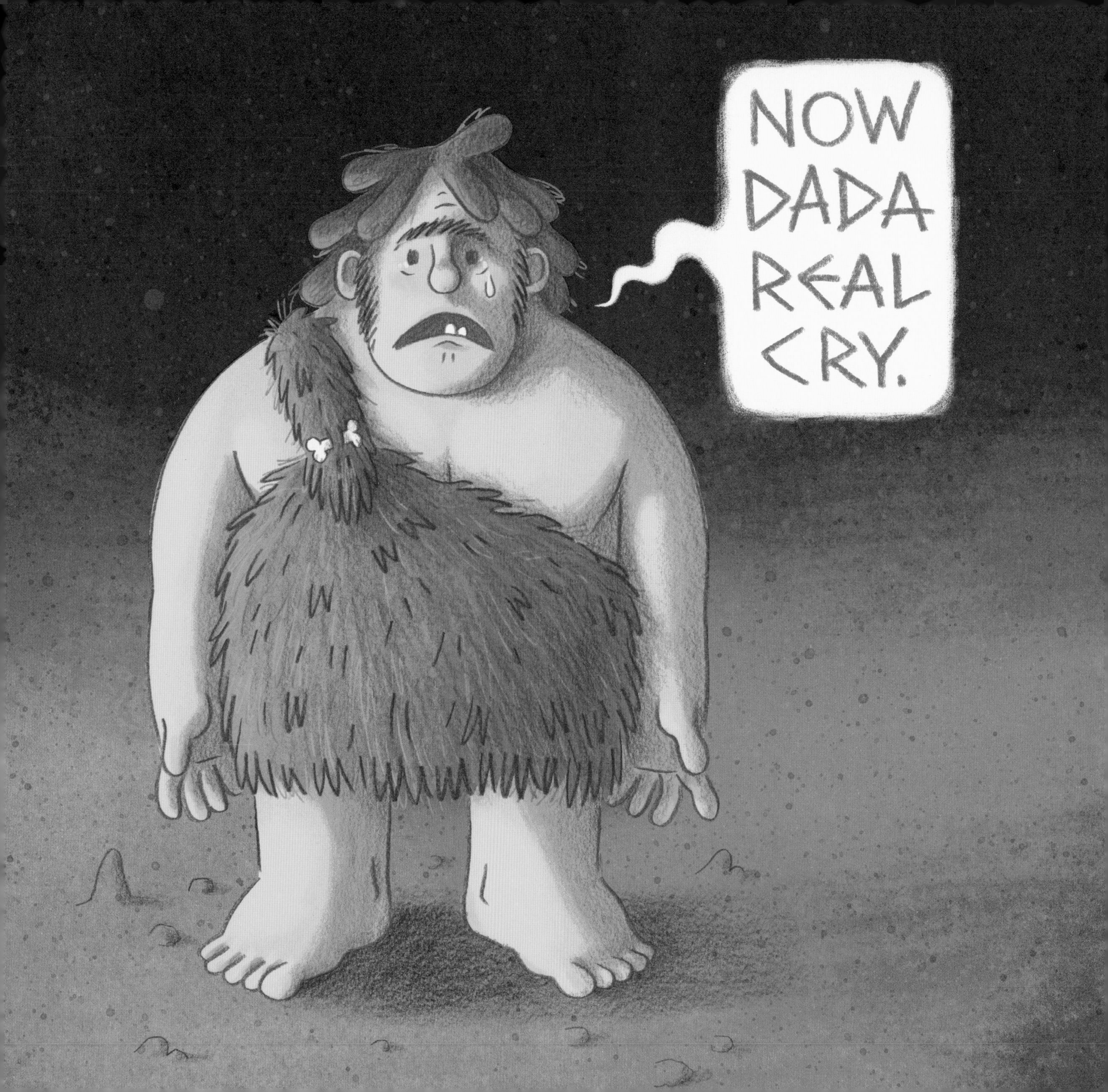
NOW DADA REAL CRY.

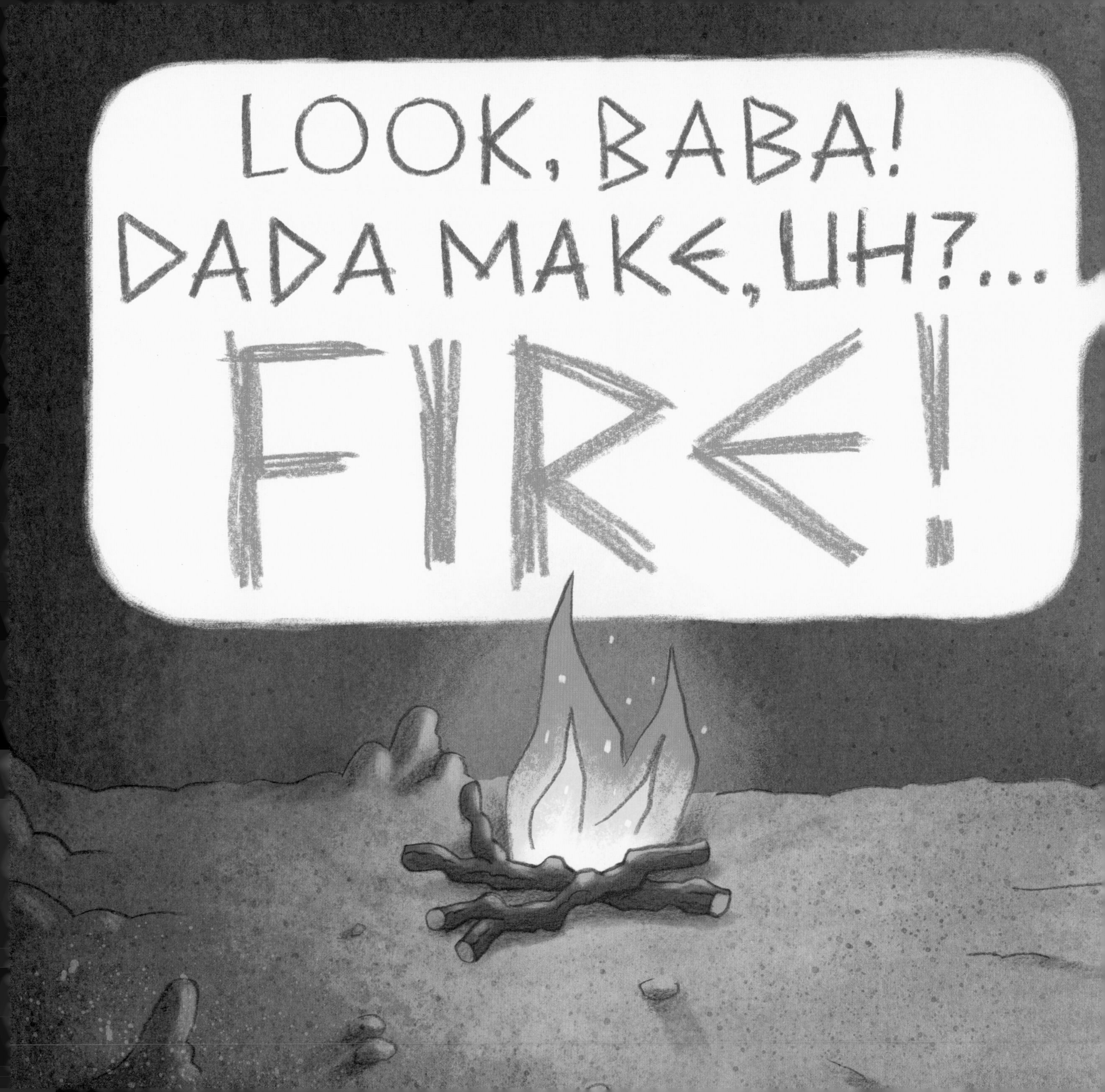
LOOK, BABA!
DADA MAKE, UH?...
FIRE!

FOR MY BROTHER, CHADD.

Copyright © 2020 by Brandon Reese.

All rights reserved. No part of this book may be
reproduced in any form without written permission
from the publisher.

Library of Congress Cataloging-in-Publication
Data available.

ISBN 978-1-4521-7994-0

Manufactured in China.

Design by Ryan Hayes and Jay Marvel.
Typeset in Gaegu.

The illustrations in this book were rendered in
colored pencil, gouache, and Adobe Photoshop.

10 9 8 7 6 5 4 3 2

Chronicle Books LLC
680 Second Street
San Francisco, California 94107

Chronicle Books—we see things differently. Become
part of our community at www.chroniclekids.com.

MIX
Paper from
responsible sources
FSC
www.fsc.org
FSC™ C008047